You can pray BIG THINGS

Julia Jeffress Sadler

Illustrated by Arief Putra

BakerBooks
a division of Baker Publishing Group
Grand Rapids, Michigan

© 2023 by Julia Jeffress Sadler

Published by Baker Books
a division of Baker Publishing Group
Grand Rapids, Michigan
BakerBooks.com

Printed in the United States of America

Library of Congress Cataloging-in-Publication Data
Names: Sadler, Julia Jeffress, 1988– author.
Title: You can pray big things / Julia Jeffress Sadler.
Description: Grand Rapids, Michigan : Baker Books, a division of Baker Publishing Group, [2023] | Audience: Ages 3–8 | Audience: Grades K–1
Identifiers: LCCN 2022049814 | ISBN 9781540902849 (cloth) | ISBN 9781493442430 (ebook)
Subjects: LCSH: Prayer—Christianity—Juvenile literature.
Classification: LCC BV210.3 .S235 2023 | DDC 248.3/2—dc23/eng/20230418
LC record available at https://lccn.loc.gov/2022049814

Baker Publishing Group publications use paper produced from sustainable forestry practices and post-consumer waste whenever possible.

23 24 25 26 27 28 29   7 6 5 4 3 2

Let each generation tell its children of your mighty acts;
   let them proclaim your power.

Psalm 145:4 (NLT)

The plans of the LORD stand firm forever,
   the purposes of his heart through all generations.

Psalm 33:11

To my wonderful parents, Amy and Robert Jeffress, who taught me as a little girl "you can pray big things!" This foundation placed a dream in my heart and a prayer in my soul that would decades later be the story of Ryan, Blair, Barrett, and Blake.

To my miracle children, I pray you will see God work as we have seen Him work! He is faithful to do more than anything you can imagine and has fought for you since before you were born.

To my amazing husband, Ryan, for all the heartfelt big prayers we have prayed together and all the ones to come!

To every parent and child reading this book, may you be inspired and encouraged that "you can pray big things!"

You can pray big things and small things
and all the in-between things,

the hard things, the happy things,
your hopes, wishes, and dreams.

No eye has seen, no ear has heard,
and no mind has imagined
what God has prepared
for those who love him.

1 Corinthians 2:9 (NLT)

Though sometimes you pray loud, and sometimes you pray soft,
no matter how loud, you can know your prayer goes off—

up past the clouds,
past the sun,
past the stars,
to the God who knows exactly who you are.

You created my inmost being;
    you knit me together in my mother's womb.
I praise you because I am fearfully and wonderfully made. . . .
Your eyes saw my unformed body;
    all the days ordained for me were written in your book
    before one of them came to be.

Psalm 139:13–14, 16

God loves to hear our prayers,
but sometimes we don't know what to pray.
For starters, you could tell God about your day.

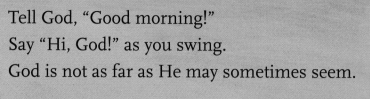

Tell God, "Good morning!"
Say "Hi, God!" as you swing.
God is not as far as He may sometimes seem.

Tell Him about your favorite food for breakfast.
Tell Him about school, about soccer, about bike-fest.

Pray in the Spirit on all occasions with
all kinds of prayers and requests.

Ephesians 6:18

When you don't know what to pray,
think of God as your friend
talking to you as He sits on the end
of your couch, in the car, on the playground, or at school.
God is right there, and He thinks you're really cool!

"I know the plans I have for you," declares the Lord, "plans to prosper you and not to harm you, plans to give you hope and a future."

Jeremiah 29:11

Pray big things—
for your dreams, for your life, for the world.
The Bible says nothing is too hard for the Lord.
God can do anything, big or small.
He loves to be near you and hear it all:

your hopes, your fears, and your funnies.
He is your best friend, so you never have to worry!
Jesus loves you, and you're going to do great things!
The sky is the limit!

Nothing will be impossible
with God.

Luke 1:37 (ESV)

Pray to be president.
Pray to win the game.
Pray to see a rainbow.
Pray to reach TV fame.
Pray to be a ballet star.
Pray your favorite team goes far.

And most of all, remember you're God's boy or girl.
You belong to Him, and He loves when you dream.
He put your dreams in your heart, as big as they may seem.

[God] is able to do
immeasurably more
than all we ask or
imagine.

Ephesians 3:20

The Bible says you can do all things through Christ who gives you strength. When you're scared or worried, remember, God thinks you're great!

God is for you, cheering you on.
This means you can hold your head high, singing His song.

I can do all this through him who
gives me strength.

Philippians 4:13

God loves when we trust Him with our hearts when things seem bad.
Sometimes our hearts can feel heavy, quiet, or sad.
We need to pray quiet prayers too—
the ones that maybe we don't want to say out loud
or in front of a crowd.

Prayer is between you and God.
Your prayer can be as soft as a whisper
that only God hears.

The LORD is close to the brokenhearted
and saves those who are crushed in spirit.
Psalm 34:18

Pray for your grandma to get well.
Pray for sickness to go away.
Pray for the friend who isn't always nice.
Pray for the test you have today.

Pray what is on your heart, little one—
no right, no wrong.
Our prayer to God is always a song,
reminding us that God is in charge, and it's not all on us.
God created the world, the stars, and is the One we can trust.

I sought the LORD, and he answered me;
he delivered me from all my fears.

Psalm 34:4

When we can't see His hand at work,
we can trust His heart.
He has been on our side from the very start!

Sometimes you pray and the answer is no.
This can seem unfair,
but you have to choose to remember that God always cares.

We know that in all things God works for the
good of those who love him, who have been
called according to his purpose.

Romans 8:28

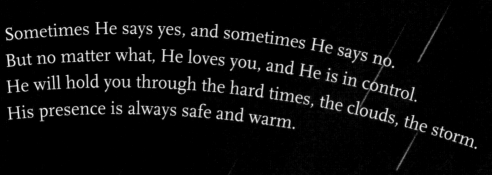

Sometimes He says yes, and sometimes He says no.
But no matter what, He loves you, and He is in control.
He will hold you through the hard times, the clouds, the storm.
His presence is always safe and warm.

We are wrapped in His arms that can't be seen but can be felt.
God is strong, brave, and mighty and is always there to help.

The LORD is a warrior;
the LORD is his name.

Exodus 15:3

Did you know God never gets tired?
He stays up all night so you can sleep.
His angel armies protect you—
you can lay down, relax, and peacefully dream.

Do not be anxious about anything, but in every situation, by prayer and petition, with thanksgiving, present your requests to God.

Philippians 4:6

When you wonder why you can't see God, remember He is like the wind:
though you can't see Him, you can feel Him,
and this gives you confidence within.

He is closer than you think, can do more than you can imagine,
and thinks you're the best of all His creation.

Look at the birds of the air; they do not sow or reap or
store away in barns, and yet your heavenly Father feeds
them. Are you not much more valuable than they?

Matthew 6:26

Did you know Jesus prays for you?
It's true!
He prays that you will know Him.
And when prayers are too hard to pray, the Holy Spirit steps in.
He turns our tears into words on those days we just can't win.

He prays for you when words won't come.
He wants you to remember God's Son.
You see, Jesus had hard times too.
He laid down His life so one day He could meet you.

In the same way, the Spirit helps us in our weakness. We do not know what we ought to pray for, but the Spirit himself intercedes for us through wordless groans. And he who searches our hearts knows the mind of the Spirit, because the Spirit intercedes for God's people in accordance with the will of God.

Romans 8:26–27

Jesus comes into our lives to change us, to save us,
to forgive us for the times we mess up.
Jesus wants to be our Lord and Savior.
And when this happens our hearts jump
with excitement, joy, love, and peace.
Jesus is ours and we know we will always be
His forever; He is our Savior and Lord.
Peace runs over and there is joy forevermore.

But just like a present isn't ours until we reach out and take it,
Jesus is waiting for us to pray to receive His gift so we can make it ours forever.
Grace is for you, His sacrifice on the cross a gift,
Jesus's present is for you, and it's the best one you'll get.

It is by grace you have been saved, through faith—
and this is not from yourselves, it is the gift of
God—not by works, so that no one can boast.

Ephesians 2:8–9

The biggest prayer of all you can pray
is one that makes sure you go to heaven one day.
God knows you, but you must know Him.
This happens by admitting you have sinned,
asking forgiveness, and inviting Jesus to come in.

God so loved the world that he gave his one and only
Son, that whoever believes in him shall not perish
but have eternal life.

John 3:16

The
Biggest
Prayer You Can Pray

Dear God,

Thank You for loving me. I know that I have sinned. And I'm truly sorry for the bad things I've done. But I believe that You loved me so much that You sent Jesus to die on the cross for my sins.

Right now, I want to pray the big prayer of trusting in Jesus and what He did for me to save me from my sins. Thank You for forgiving me. Please help me to live the rest of my life obeying You. In Jesus's name I pray. Amen.

If you declare with your mouth, "Jesus is Lord," and believe in your heart that God raised him from the dead, you will be saved. For it is with your heart that you believe and are justified, and it is with your mouth that you profess your faith and are saved.

Romans 10:9–10

A Note to Parents

Thank you for teaching your children to pray big things to God! Praying is fun and imaginative, and it helps children communicate their feelings, fears, and dreams to God and to you. As a therapist and minister, I wanted to include how to process when the answer to our prayers is no and things don't turn out how we want them to. My prayer is this book helps give words to your child's thoughts and the language of "pray big things" becomes common in your home.

Jesus loves little children. He says in Matthew 19:14, "Let the little children come to me, and do not hinder them, for the kingdom of heaven belongs to such as these." I could not write this book without also including the biggest prayer of all: the salvation prayer that I prayed as a five-year-old to accept Christ as my Savior. While not every child reading this may be ready to make that commitment, many of them will be! If you have never asked forgiveness for your sins and asked Jesus to be your personal Lord and Savior, then I hope you will pray this big prayer today.

The biblical truth that God hears us when we pray, genuinely cares, and is able to do "more than all we ask or imagine" will be written on your child's heart and mind and will guide them all their life (Ephesians 3:20). Thank you for faithfully telling the little ones in your life, "You can pray big things!"